KATIE KAZOO, SWITCHEROO

Quiet on the Set!

by Nancy Krulik • illustrated by John & Wendy

Grosset & Dunlap

For Danny, my superstar!—N.K.

For Susan, who is shy,
even to her friends—J&W

Text copyright © 2003 by Nancy Krulik. Illustrations copyright © 2003 by
John and Wendy. All rights reserved. Published by Grosset & Dunlap, a
division of Penguin Young Readers Group, 345 Hudson Street, New York,
New York, 10014. Printed in the U.S.A.

Library of Congress Cataloging-in-Publication Data

Krulik, Nancy E.
  Quiet on the set! / by Nancy Krulik ; illustrated by John & Wendy.
    p. cm. — (Katie Kazoo, Switcheroo ; 10)
Summary: While a movie is being filmed in Cherrydale, Katie switches into
Rosie Moran, a world renowned child actress.
  ISBN 0-448-43214-5 (pbk.)
  [1. Child actors—Fiction. 2. Actors and actresses—Fiction. 3. Magic—
Fiction.] I. John & Wendy. II. Title.
  PZ7.K9416Qu 2003
  [Fic]—dc22
                                                            2003017968
          ISBN 0-448-43214-5   G H I J

Chapter 1

"Extra, extra! Read all about it!" Jeremy Fox shouted. "Speedy Escapes!"

"Ooh! You've got the new *3A Times*," Katie Carew said as she took a copy of the newspaper.

"I publish a paper every week," Jeremy told his best friend. "That's the editor's job."

"And you're so good at it," Becky Stern said. "This is the greatest newspaper in the whole school."

Jeremy blushed. He knew Becky liked him—*everyone* knew it. But that didn't mean Jeremy liked her back.

Jeremy turned to Katie. "I think you'll like this article. It's about Speedy."

Katie loved all animals. Her favorite animal was her cocker spaniel, Pepper. But she liked Speedy, the class hamster, too.

George Brennan and Kevin Camilleri raced over to Jeremy. Kevin seemed especially happy to see the new edition of the *3A Times.*

"Did you write about how I was the one who rescued Speedy?" Kevin asked.

"You didn't exactly rescue him," Jeremy said. "He was sitting in the salad bar eating lettuce. You just picked him up and carried him back to the classroom."

Kevin frowned. "Well, if I hadn't gone back to the salad bar for more tomatoes, no one would have found Speedy. We would never have seen him again."

Becky got a funny look on her face. "I'm never going to eat at the salad bar again. Who knows what that hamster did in there!"

"Ooh, that *is* gross," Jeremy agreed.

Sharing the salad bar with Speedy didn't seem to bother Kevin. "No one—not even Speedy—is going to keep me from my tomatoes!" he declared.

"Kevin's right," George said. "Nothing Speedy did could be worse than the big bug I found in my cake last week."

"You found a bug in your cake?" Katie asked.

George nodded. "I guess it was the fly's day off!" He started laughing.

Katie giggled. She loved George's jokes.

"Hi, you guys!" Suzanne Lock shouted as she dashed across the playground to join the other kids in class 3A.

Suzanne was wearing a long green skirt, suede boots, and a shimmery pink shirt. Her hair was piled high on her head. She looked like she was going to a fancy party.

"Wow, you look so cool!" Katie said, complimenting her.

Suzanne grinned. "Thanks."

"Why are you dressed so fancy?" Becky asked.

"It's my current events day," Suzanne told her.

"Is that all?" George said. "You don't have

to get all dressed up to do your current events. I never do."

"Me, neither," Kevin agreed. "I don't dress up for anything."

"Well, *I* try to look good all the time," Suzanne told them. "You never know when a movie producer could be looking for a new star."

Jeremy rolled his eyes. Sometimes Suzanne really annoyed him. This was one of those times. Jeremy and Suzanne were both Katie's best friends, but that didn't mean they liked each other very much.

"What are you talking about, Suzanne?" Jeremy asked her.

"You'll find out," Suzanne assured him. "It's part of my current events report. And I guarantee my news will beat anything in the *3A Times*!"

Chapter 2

Katie sat in the classroom and stared at the clock. It was only 11:33. She tried to focus on the problems in her math textbook. But her eyes kept going back to the numbers on the clock. Katie couldn't wait for 11:45. That was current events time. She was dying to find out what Suzanne's news story was.

The other kids were having trouble waiting for current events time, too. Everyone seemed to be watching the clock . . . and Suzanne.

Katie knew Suzanne was happy everyone was watching her. There were two things Suzanne really loved—being the center of

attention, and knowing something no one else knew. Today, Suzanne had both of those things.

Finally, Mrs. Derkman put away her math textbook, and took a seat behind her big desk in the front of the room.

"Okay, class, whose turn is it for current events?"

"Suzanne's!" everyone shouted out at once.

Suzanne stood up and walked slowly toward the front of the room.

"Come on, Suzanne, tell us what the big deal is," George said as she walked past his desk.

"Yeah, what's this great news you have for us?" Kevin added.

But Suzanne didn't hurry. She liked making everyone wait for her surprise.

"Okay," she said, taking a dramatic breath. "Here's the big story. Some famous Hollywood producers are making a movie in Cherrydale."

"Why would anyone make a movie here?"

George asked. "There's nothing special about Cherrydale."

"That's the point," Suzanne said. "They wanted an average American town. And you guys haven't heard the best part. This movie stars Rosie Moran!"

Rosie Moran was the most famous kid in the whole world. She was a big movie star, even though she was only nine years old. The kids had all seen her movies.

So had Mrs. Derkman. "I love Rosie Moran!" the teacher blurted out.

"You go to Rosie Moran movies?" George asked her, surprised.

Mrs. Derkman nodded. "I've seen *all* her movies. *Camp Capers, Camp Capers 2,* and *Sleepover Summer*. But my favorite Rosie Moran movie is her first one— *Scary School Day*."

Suzanne continued her report. "The name of the movie is *The Kids Are in Charge*. In this movie, the parents in a small town switch places with their kids. The adults go to school, and the kids go to work."

"Oh, that sounds marvelous!" Mrs. Derkman gushed. "I can just see Rosie Moran playing the head of a big company. Or a firefighter. Ooh! Maybe they'll let her play a teacher!"

Katie didn't think the movie sounded marvelous. She thought it sounded awful. Katie didn't like anything that had to do with switching places.

That was because Katie had done a lot of switching recently.

It had all started one day a few weeks ago. Katie had spilled mud on her favorite jeans, lost the football game for her team, and let out a massive burp in front of the entire class.

On that day, Katie had wished she could be anyone but herself.

There must have been a shooting star flying overhead when she made that wish, because the very next day, the magic wind came. The magic wind was a wild tornado that blew only around Katie. It was so strong that it had the power to turn Katie into someone else.

The first time the magic wind came, it turned Katie into Speedy, the class hamster. She'd spent the whole morning gnawing on chew sticks, running on the hamster wheel, and trying to escape from Speedy's cage. She was so glad when the magic wind returned and turned her back into Katie Carew.

But Katie hadn't stayed herself for very long. The magic wind came back again and again. It had already turned her into other kids, like Suzanne's baby sister Heather, Becky Stern, and Jeremy Fox. One time, the magic wind turned her into Mr. Kane, the school principal. Another time, it turned her into Lucille, the lunch lady in the cafeteria.

Katie never knew when the magic wind would come back again. All Katie knew was that when it did, she was going to wind up getting into some sort of trouble—and so would the person she'd turn into.

That's why Katie didn't think a movie about kids who switch places with adults would be very good. There was nothing funny about switcheroos.

Chapter 3

Katie might not have thought that *The Kids Are in Charge* sounded like a good movie, but the other kids sure were excited. It was all they could talk about at lunch.

"Today, they're filming a scene on Main Street, in front of the pet shop," Suzanne told the kids at their lunch table. "My mother said I could go there after school. I hope I can meet the director."

"I hope I can meet Rosie Moran," Mrs. Derkman interrupted.

The kids all looked up in shock. Mrs. Derkman never sat with them at lunch. But there she was, putting her lunch tray down beside Kevin.

Kevin moved his chair as far as he could away from the teacher.

"I've heard Rosie's just like a normal kid," Mandy Banks said.

"My magazine says she likes skating and guitar," Miriam added.

"I read that her favorite color is blue," Mrs. Derkman chimed in.

The kids all stared at her.

"Katie, do you want to come to Main Street with me?" Suzanne asked.

Katie didn't want to be anywhere near *The Kids Are in Charge*—in case it gave the magic wind any ideas. But she couldn't explain that to Suzanne. So she said, "I guess I can go for a little while."

After school, Katie and her friends headed over to Main Street.

"Wow! Would you look at this!" Jeremy exclaimed.

"I've never seen Main Street this busy!" Katie added.

Usually, Main Street was a quiet place, with people walking down the sidewalk and a few cars parked on the street. But today people with walkie-talkies ran on the sidewalk. Big trucks with lights were parked near the pet shop. And everywhere you looked there were huge trailers.

"Those are the stars' dressing rooms," Suzanne told her friends.

"I wonder which trailer belongs to Rosie Moran?" Miriam asked as the kids tried to peek inside the windows.

Suddenly a man in a black leather jacket jumped in front of Katie and her friends. "You kids have to wait here. They're about to film the next scene."

"Right now?" Suzanne asked excitedly.

The man in the jacket nodded. "Any second now Rosie is going to walk out of that pet shop and onto the street. If you're real quiet you can watch."

The kids all stared at the door of the pet shop. A woman stood in front of the shop with a big black clapboard. "Scene twelve, take three," she said. Then she opened the top of the board and clapped it down.

Rosie Moran walked out of the pet shop. She looked like she was about to cry. "I wish Mr. Marks was here. He'd know what to do," she said. A tear fell down her cheek.

"And . . . cut!" the director shouted. "That was perfect, Rosie."

"Thank goodness," Rosie moaned. "I don't want to have to cry again today." She turned and ran toward her trailer. But before she could reach the door, Miriam jumped in front of her.

"Rosie, I'm your biggest fan," Miriam gushed. "Can I have your autograph?"

Rosie shook her head. Her long chocolate brown curls bounced all around her. "Get out of my way."

Miriam looked as though she'd been slapped across the face. "But I just want your autograph. I love all your movies."

"Everyone says that," Rosie snapped back. "Can't you come up with anything more original?"

"The magazines all said you were nice," Miriam sobbed.

"Don't believe everything you read," Rosie shouted. She stormed into her trailer and slammed the door.

Chapter 4

As the kids stood on the sidewalk, they could hear Rosie shouting from inside her trailer. "I told them not to let anyone on the set!" she screamed. "How am I supposed to think with all those kids around?"

Miriam sobbed harder.

"Don't cry," Katie urged her classmate. "She's not worth it."

"I'm never going to see any of her movies again," Mandy promised.

"None of us will," Jeremy said.

Suzanne looked at her classmates. "I'll see this movie," she told them.

The kids all stared at Suzanne with surprise.

"I'll see it if I get to be in it," Suzanne explained.

George laughed. "Guess you won't be seeing it, either, then."

Suzanne stuck her tongue out at him.

Just then a woman with dark, short hair and glasses burst out of Rosie's dressing room. "I'm really sorry about that," she apologized. "Rosie is usually so nice to her fans. She's a little cranky today."

Katie frowned. A little cranky? Rosie had been *mean*!

"I just spoke to her," the woman continued. "She's sorry."

"Are you Rosie's mother?" Katie asked.

"Oh, no. I'm Amy Edmunds, Rosie's assistant," the woman explained kindly. "Rosie would really like to make it up to you. In fact, she's on the phone right now, asking the director to let all of you be extras in the movie."

Jeremy looked at her curiously. "Extra whats?" he asked.

Suzanne rolled her eyes. "You'll have to forgive him," she said. "He doesn't know anything about the *biz*."

"Oh, and you do?" Jeremy asked.

"I know that extras are actors who stand in the background to make the scene look real," Suzanne told him.

"Exactly," Amy agreed. "Rosie would like you all to be extras in the scene we're filming Saturday." She pulled some papers from her clipboard. "Have your parents sign these permission slips. Be at the park on Saturday morning."

Just then, Mrs. Derkman came running over. "Did you kids meet Rosie Moran?" the teacher asked excitedly.

"We met her, all right." George frowned.

"Was she just like we expected?" Mrs. Derkman continued.

"Not exactly," Katie began.

"She's *better* than we expected," Suzanne interrupted excitedly. "She invited us all to be extras in *The Kids Are in Charge*!"

"How wonderful!" Mrs. Derkman exclaimed. She turned to Amy Edmunds. "Is there room for one more?" she asked.

Amy shook her head. "Sorry, kids only."

Mrs. Derkman looked like she was about to cry!

Chapter 5

That evening, Katie and her mother went to the Cherrydale Mall to the Book Nook bookstore, where Katie's mom works. There was a big shipment of books coming in, and Mrs. Carew had to make sure they were all put out on the right shelves.

"Why don't you go to Louie's Pizza Shop?" Katie's mom said. "You can do your homework there."

Katie smiled. Math homework wouldn't be so awful if she could do it while she bit into Louie's secret sauce and extra gooey cheese. "See you later," she called to her mom.

"Hi, Katie," Louie said as Katie walked

into the pizza shop. "Is your mom working tonight?"

Katie nodded. "She said I should wait for her here."

"It's crowded, but I think you can find a table in the back," Louie told Katie. "I'll bring you a slice in a minute."

"Thanks, Louie," Katie said.

Katie sat down and took out her math book. She tried hard to concentrate, but the people at the table behind her were having a loud argument.

"This just isn't a good time," one woman said.

"But it's what she wants," the other woman argued.

"I'm her mother. I know what's best for her!" the first woman shouted.

"Why are you two talking about me like I'm not around?" the girl at the table said.

Katie's eyes flew open wide. She'd know that voice anywhere. The girl sitting behind her was Rosie Moran!

"Mom, I don't want to quit acting. I love acting. But I need a break," Rosie pleaded. "I want to be a normal kid for once. At least for a little while."

"You're *not* a normal kid," Rosie's mother argued. "You're a star. Besides, you have to finish this movie. I've already signed the contract."

Rosie leaped up from the table and ran sobbing into the bathroom.

Katie had been mad at Rosie for the way she'd treated Miriam. But now she felt really sorry for her. Quickly, she followed Rosie into the bathroom.

The bathroom looked empty. But Katie could hear sniffling coming from one of the stalls.

"Are you okay?" Katie called out.

"Go away," Rosie snapped back.

"I just thought you could use a friend," Katie answered.

"I don't have any friends."

"Sure you do," Katie said. "I'll be your friend."

Slowly, Rosie opened the door to the stall. "Weren't you one of the kids on the set today?" she asked Katie.

Katie nodded.

"So why do you want to be friends with me? I wasn't very nice."

"That's true," Katie agreed. "But everybody gets in a bad mood sometimes."

"I'm in a bad mood a lot," Rosie admitted.

"Maybe you're working too hard. I get that way when I have too much homework," Katie said.

"I don't have any homework," Rosie told her.

"Don't you go to school?" Katie asked.

"Sort of," Rosie explained. "I have a tutor. She teaches me when I'm on the set."

"Just you?" Katie asked. "No other kids?"

Rosie nodded. "It's just me and her. But I wish I went to school like you. I'll bet it's fun."

Katie thought about that. Mrs. Derkman's classroom wasn't always a fun place to be. But at least there was lunchtime and recess.

Just then, Katie got a great idea. "How long are you going to be in Cherrydale?" she asked Rosie.

"Until Sunday," Rosie answered.

"Well, how about coming to my school for the rest of the week?" Katie asked her.

Rosie shook her head. "I can't just go to a school for one week," she said. "Your teacher wouldn't let me."

Katie thought about how Mrs. Derkman had spent the whole day talking about Rosie Moran. "I'll bet she would," she assured Rosie.

"It would be a lot of fun," Rosie admitted.

"Then it's a deal," Katie said. "Meet me at Cherrydale Elementary School tomorrow morning."

"Okay," Rosie agreed.

Katie started to leave.

"Hey," Rosie called after her. "I don't even know your name."

"It's Katie Carew," Katie told her. "But you can call me Katie Kazoo. All my friends do."

"Okay, *Katie,*" Rosie told her. "I'll see you tomorrow."

Chapter 6

"Do you really think she'll come?" Suzanne asked Katie as the two girls sat in the school playground early the next morning.

"I hope so," Katie told her.

Just then, a big black limousine pulled up in the school parking lot.

"She's here!" Katie shouted.

A tall man in a blue uniform leaped out of the driver's seat of the limo. He opened the back door and stood to the side. Rosie got out of the car.

"Thanks, Frank," she said to the driver. "School's over at three o'clock. You can come get me then."

"Very good, Miss Moran," Frank said.

As Frank drove away, Rosie walked toward the bench where Katie and Suzanne were sitting.

"Hi, Katie Kazoo," she greeted Katie.

"Hi, Rosie," Katie replied. "I'm so glad you could come. I thought maybe your mother wouldn't let you."

"She almost didn't. But I convinced her that we could tell some of the fan magazines about my time in regular school. She liked that."

"Ahem!" Suzanne interrupted. "Aren't you forgetting something, Katie?"

Katie blushed. "Oh, I'm sorry. Rosie, this is Suzanne Lock."

"Nice to meet you, Suzanne," Rosie said.

"I think we'll be good friends," Suzanne told her. "We have a lot in common."

"We do?" Rosie asked.

"Sure," Suzanne assured her. "We're both actresses."

"Cool!" Rosie said. "What kind of acting do you do? Movies or the stage?"

Suzanne blushed. "Well, nothing yet. But I'm on the verge of getting an acting job."

"Oh, right," Katie remembered. "We're all going to be extras in your new movie," she said to Rosie.

"Well, that's just a start," Suzanne said. "I meant bigger parts, of course."

"I'm sure you're a great actress," Rosie assured Suzanne. Then she turned to Katie. "Are you sure your teacher won't mind having me in class for a few days?"

"Oh, no," Katie assured her. "I asked her all about it last night."

Rosie seemed confused. "You saw your teacher last night?" she asked.

Katie nodded. "She's my next door neighbor."

"Your teacher is your neighbor!" Rosie exclaimed. "That's really cool."

Suzanne laughed. "Cool is not a word I would use to describe Mrs. Derkman."

"Oh," Rosie said. "What is she like?"

"See for yourself." Katie pointed across the playground. Mrs. Derkman was running across the pavement.

Katie and Suzanne stared at their teacher. They'd never even seen her walk fast before, never mind run.

"Yoo-hoo! Rosie!" Mrs. Derkman shouted. "Hello."

Rosie jumped to her feet. "Hello," she said quietly.

"Oh, I can hardly believe you're here," Mrs. Derkman exclaimed. "You're even more beautiful in real life. And I love the outfit you're wearing."

Suzanne and Katie studied Rosie's clothes. She was wearing black stretch jeans, a leopard pattern shirt, and a leather jacket with fringe. She did look pretty cool.

"I think that's probably the most fashionable thing anyone has ever worn at Cherrydale Elementary School," Mrs. Derkman gushed.

Suzanne let out a tiny gasp.

"You look fantastic, too, Suzanne," Katie interrupted, trying to soothe her friend. "I love that headband. And your shoes are really cool."

But nothing could make Suzanne feel

better. She glared angrily at Rosie.

"Well, I see the other children are coming," Mrs. Derkman told Rosie. "Why don't we line up and get an early start? It would be terrific to get a couple of extra minutes of learning in this morning."

"Okay." Rosie smiled at Mrs. Derkman.

"Just what we need, extra learning time," Suzanne hissed as Rosie and Mrs. Derkman walked off together.

"It's not her fault," Katie said.

"No, it's not," Suzanne agreed. "It's yours."

"Mine?" Katie asked.

"You invited her here," Suzanne reminded her.

"Come on, it's no big deal," Katie said. "Besides, you wanted Rosie to come today, too."

"I don't know, Katie," Suzanne said as she stared at Rosie's leather jacket and stretch jeans. "I think this was a bad idea."

Chapter 7

"Rosie, why don't you sit in the empty desk in the first row?" Mrs. Derkman suggested.

Rosie sat down next to Jeremy and smiled. Jeremy blushed.

"Okay, class, let's go back to talking about verbs. Everybody pull out your grammar books," Mrs. Derkman said.

Rosie raised her hand shyly. "I don't have any books," she said.

"You can share with Jeremy," the teacher answered.

It was easy to see that Jeremy was excited to share his book with a movie star!

Becky's face burned red. She didn't like

that Rosie was sharing with Jeremy. She
especially didn't like how glad Jeremy was to
do it.

"Who can tell me what a verb is?" Mrs.
Derkman asked.

Kevin raised his hand. "It's an action
word . . ." he began.

Before Kevin could finish his sentence,
Rosie began to sing. "Herb the Verb is a man
of action. He's busy all day through. He hops
and walks, giggles and talks. He does what-
ever we do."

Everyone in the class stared at Rosie. They waited for Mrs. Derkman to yell at her.

But Mrs. Derkman didn't yell. Instead, she said, "What a lovely song."

"There's a dance that goes with it," Rosie told her.

The class watched with amazement as Rosie began to hop around the room. When she reached the front of the room again, she did a flip in the air, and landed on one leg.

Mrs. Derkman applauded. "Isn't it exciting to have such a talented gymnast visit us?" Mrs. Derkman asked the class.

Now Becky was *really* angry. She'd been studying gymnastics since she was a little girl. She was a lot better than Rosie.

"That looks like fun!" George jumped up and twirled in a circle. He bent his knee and stuck his leg out behind him. "Look at me! I'm Herb the Verb!"

The class laughed. George looked like the world's goofiest ballerina.

"George!" Mrs. Derkman exclaimed. "Take your seat immediately."

"How come she gets to dance?" he asked the teacher.

"Rosie was teaching us a way to remember what a verb is," the teacher replied. "You're just being silly. Now sit down, or you will lose recess today."

George plopped down in his chair. He had a very grumpy look on his face.

"How much longer is she staying here?" he hissed angrily at Katie.

Chapter 8

At lunchtime, Katie walked with Rosie to the cafeteria.

"You eat here every day?" Rosie asked Katie with a frown.

"Sure."

"It's not what I expected," Rosie said, looking around. "I thought it would be more like the restaurant at the movie studio."

"What's that like?" Katie asked.

"Well, there are a lot of tables, and you get your food on line, like here," Rosie said. "But it's decorated with flowers and plants. There are cloth napkins and real silverware, not plastic. And the food smells a lot better."

"Well, you wanted to go to a real school," Katie reminded her. "This is real school food."

Rosie smiled. "You're right. It *is* fun here," she told Katie. "And your teacher is *so* nice."

Katie raised her eyebrow, but she didn't say anything. Nice was not a word most kids would use to describe Mrs. Derkman. Then again, Mrs. Derkman was treating Rosie a lot differently than she treated the rest of her students.

After the girls had loaded their trays with macaroni and cheese, chocolate pudding, and milk, they walked over toward a table in the corner. Some of the kids from class 3A were already sitting there.

"Katie, I saved you a seat!" Suzanne called out.

"Squeeze over," Katie asked Suzanne. "Rosie needs to sit, too."

"Sorry, no room," Suzanne said. "She can sit over there." Suzanne pointed toward the other side of the table where Jeremy was sitting.

"It's okay, Katie," Rosie said. "I don't mind."

But before Rosie could sit down, Becky moved to the seat next to Jeremy.

Rosie shrugged and sat down where Becky had been sitting. That put her right across from George.

"Rosie, maybe you don't want to . . ." Katie began. She wanted to

warn her not to sit near George. He could be really gross at lunch.

"Leave her alone," Suzanne interrupted. "Serves her right."

Everyone started eating. Everyone but George, that is. He was busy rolling pieces of bread into little balls. He launched one of the bread balls toward the end of the table. It landed right on top of Miriam's macaroni.

"Ooh! Gross. You rolled that ball in your dirty fingers," Miriam moaned. "Now how am I supposed to eat my lunch?"

George threw a bread ball at Kevin. Kevin didn't think the ball was gross. He picked it

up off the table and popped it in his mouth.

Suzanne and Miriam looked like they were going to throw up. But Rosie wasn't grossed out at all. "He's funny," Rosie said.

"George is the funniest guy in our whole class," Kevin told her. "Maybe even in our whole school."

George smiled proudly.

"You like jokes?" Rosie asked him.

George nodded.

"Have you heard this one?" Rosie asked. "What kind of star wears fancy sunglasses and drives an expensive car?"

"I don't know," George said.

"A movie star!" Rosie joked. She started to laugh.

So did Kevin. "That's pretty funny," he said. "It looks like George has some competition."

George frowned and threw another ball of bread at Kevin.

Kevin picked up the bread ball and got ready to throw it back at George. But before he could, Mrs. Derkman arrived at the table. "Are you kids playing soccer after lunch?" the teacher asked.

Jeremy nodded. "We're playing against the kids in class 3B."

"Who are the captains?" Mrs. Derkman asked.

"Jeremy and Andrew Epstein," Kevin told her.

Mrs. Derkman thought about that for a moment. "Why don't we let our guest be the captain of our team today?"

"Jeremy is our best player," Becky said, butting in.

"Yes," Mrs. Derkman agreed. "But I'll bet Rosie has never been a soccer captain."

"I've never even *played* soccer," Rosie admitted.

"Well, today you'll play," Mrs. Derkman assured her. "I'm sure you'll make a great captain."

As the teacher walked away, Jeremy turned

to Kevin. "Oh, great," he complained. "A captain who doesn't even know how to play. We're going to lose for sure." Jeremy glared at Rosie. He hated losing.

"Katie, why did you have to invite her to our school?" Suzanne whispered. "She's ruining everything!"

"Shhh," Katie warned. "She'll hear you."

But Rosie had already heard Suzanne. She jumped up from the table and ran toward the bathroom. Katie followed right behind her.

"Funny how we keep meeting in bathrooms," Katie joked as the two girls stood alone by the sinks.

Rosie didn't smile. "This is all your fault!" she yelled at Katie.

"What is?"

"The kids all hate me," Rosie told her.

"No, they don't," Katie said. " It's just hard being the new kid. George went through the same thing when he moved here. Becky did, too."

Rosie sobbed. "My mother was right. I can't be a normal kid."

"Sure you can," Katie assured her. "You just have to stay at a school for more than a few days. Then you'll become just one of the kids."

"I'm never going to have friends."

"But I'm your friend," Katie reminded her.

"No, you're not," Rosie said. "This is the

worst day of my whole life, and you did it to me!" She stormed out of the bathroom.

After school, Rosie got into her big limo and drove away. She never even waved good-bye.

"I hope we never see her again," George said.

"Yeah," Jeremy agreed. "We got killed in soccer today."

"I'll see her again," Suzanne said.

"You will?" Katie asked. "I thought you hated her."

"I do," Suzanne agreed. "But I'm still going to be in her movie."

"Suzanne . . ." Katie started.

"Oh, come on, Katie. We have to go to the set on Saturday."

"*We?*" Katie asked.

"Sure." Suzanne threw her arm around Katie. "I want my best friend there when I become a star!"

Chapter 9

On Saturday morning, Katie and Suzanne walked over to the park together. Katie was wearing a pair of purple jeans with laces on the side, and a white shirt. Suzanne was wearing a shimmery blue dress, long, dangly earrings, and a feather boa.

"I thought we were supposed to wear our regular clothes," Katie said.

"These are my regular clothes," Suzanne argued.

"That boa is from last Halloween," Katie reminded her. "And you wore that dress to your cousin's wedding."

"So what? I'm a star. I want the director to

notice me right away."

Katie looked at Suzanne's big earrings and her feather boa. "Oh, he'll notice you," she assured her.

Suzanne lifted her head high. "Oh, and one thing," she told Katie. "If the director asks, my name isn't Suzanne Lock."

"It isn't?"

Suzanne shook her head. "From now on I'm Suzanne Superstar!"

"You changed your name?"

Suzanne nodded. "It's my stage name. All us movie stars have them."

The other kids were already on the set by the time Suzanne and Katie got to the park. Like Suzanne, they didn't care how much they disliked Rosie. They just wanted to be in a movie!

Becky, Miriam, and Mandy were looking at the giant cameras and lights. Jeremy was kicking a can around the park. George and

Kevin were at the food table. Rosie was sitting on the steps of her trailer. She did not want to talk to any of the kids from class 3A.

"Okay, everyone, let's get started," a tall man in a baseball cap called out. "I'm Carl Swenson, the director of this movie."

Carl looked out at the kids in front of him. His eyes stopped at Suzanne. "What are you wearing?" he asked her.

"This old thing?" Suzanne asked sweetly. "It's just something I pulled from my closet. Do you like it?"

Carl shook his head. "It's all wrong. Run over to the green trailer and see if there's something the costume people have for you."

Katie thought that would make Suzanne mad. But Suzanne seemed really happy.

"I'm getting a costume!" she whispered excitedly to Katie.

After a few minutes, Suzanne came out of the trailer. She did not look happy anymore. Suzanne was dressed in a pair of old overalls.

She looked very regular.

"Now we can begin," Carl said. "You kids walk around and pretend to enjoy the day. Then Rosie will come out and say her lines. Everybody understand?"

The children nodded.

"Good," Carl said. "Let's shoot the scene."

A woman with a clapboard stood in front of the camera. "Park scene, take one," she said.

Katie and her friends walked quietly around the park, looking at the trees and smiling at each other. Then Rosie walked in front of the camera. She looked beautiful in her short green dress. Her makeup made her eyes look even bigger and bluer than usual.

Rosie opened her mouth to speak. Suzanne did a flying leap across the grass, and landed right beside her.

"Cut!" Carl shouted. He turned to Suzanne. "What did you do?"

"My character is a dancer," Suzanne explained sweetly. "She's flying through the air to celebrate this day."

Carl's face turned red. "Your character is a normal, everyday kid. There's no dancing . . . uh . . . what's your name?" he asked.

"Suzanne Superstar," Suzanne answered.

"More like Super*weird*," George joked.

Everyone laughed. Even Rosie.

"Let's try this again," Carl said. "Action!"

Once again the kids walked around the park. Rosie stepped in front of the camera.

"Hi, there!" Suzanne yelled out. "Isn't this a gorgeous day?"

"Cut!" Carl shouted. "What are you doing? You're an extra. Extras don't speak."

"It isn't normal for kids to be quiet in the park," Suzanne corrected him. "I was trying to help make it more real."

Carl's face was really red now. "You know how you can help?" he shouted.

"How?" Suzanne asked eagerly.

"You can leave."

Suzanne stared at him. "What?" she asked.

"You can leave," he repeated. "Every minute we waste costs the studio thousands of dollars. I can't afford to keep stopping for you. You're fired."

Suzanne's eyes opened wide. She turned

beet red, and started to cry. Then she raced off the set.

Katie ran after her. "Wait up," she said as she ran into a wooded part of the park. But Suzanne was too fast. Before Katie could reach her, Suzanne was out of the park and on her way home.

Katie stood there, all alone in the woods. Suddenly, she felt a cool wind blowing on the back of her neck. Katie looked up at the trees. The leaves were still. She looked down at the grass. Not a blade was moving.

Oh, no! The magic wind was back.

Within seconds, the wind was swirling around her like a giant tornado. Katie felt like she could be blown away. Quickly, she grabbed on to a tree and shut her eyes tightly.

And then it stopped. Just like that.

Slowly, Katie opened her eyes and looked around. She was still in the park.

Okay, so now she knew where she was. But she didn't know *who* she was.

Just then a woman with a clipboard and a walkie-talkie came up beside her. "I've found her," she said into her walkie-talkie. Then she turned to Katie. "You'd better hurry back, Rosie," she said. "Carl's getting really mad!"

Chapter 10

Before Katie knew what was going on, the woman with the clipboard was dragging her back onto the movie set.

"But I can't . . ." Katie began. Then she stopped herself. She couldn't tell this woman that she wasn't really Rosie Moran. She would never believe her. Katie wouldn't believe it either if it weren't happening to her.

"Rosie's back," Carl said as Katie stood in front of the camera. "Let's get to work, people. Time is money! Makeup, get rid of that shine on her nose!"

A man jumped in front of Katie. He pushed a big powder puff in her face. Chalky white powder flew in her mouth and up her nose. Katie coughed hard.

Before Katie could catch her breath, a woman snapped a clapboard right in front of her. "Park scene, take three!"

"Action!" Carl shouted.

Katie gulped. She didn't know what to do. She didn't know how to be a movie star. The only thing she'd ever seen stars do was walk down the red carpet before awards shows.

So, that's what Katie did. She raised her head high, smiled at the camera, and waved at imaginary fans. Then she spun around in a circle, showing her make-believe gown to the invisible photographers.

"Cut!" Carl yelled. "What are you doing?"

Katie shrugged. "I'm acting like a movie star."

"Why?"

"Because I *am* a movie star. I'm Rosie Moran."

Carl sighed. "In real life, you are. But in

this movie, you're just a kid. Now say your line and we can move on."

Katie gulped. She had no idea what Rosie's line was. "I don't know what to say," she admitted.

"No, no, no!" Carl yelled. "The line is, 'I do wish I could go back in time and reverse things'."

Katie wrinkled her nose. "That's what I'm supposed to say?"

Carl nodded.

"But no kid talks like that."

"You do in this film," Carl barked at her. "And . . . action!"

Katie smiled brightly into the camera. "I do wish I could go back in time and reverse things," she said.

Carl's face turned bright red. "No! No! No!" he shouted.

"I said the line," Katie told him.

"True," Carl admitted angrily. "But why are you smiling?"

Katie had never heard a grown-up yell so loudly. Her eyes welled up with tears.

"That's better," Carl said. "I want to see crying. Lots of crying."

A tear dripped down Katie's cheek.

"Perfect," Carl said. "Keep going. Action!"

Katie cried so hard that her nose began to run. She wiped it with her sleeve.

"Cut!" Carl screamed.

"That's disgusting. Somebody get Rosie a tissue!"

Katie sobbed harder.

Carl turned to the cameraman. "My agent warned me not to work with kids," he said.

"Can I try it again?" Katie whispered.

"Do we have a choice?" Carl barked back.

The makeup man shoved the powder puff in Katie's face again.

The woman with the clapboard shouted, "Park scene, take six."

"Action!" Carl ordered.

Katie opened her mouth to speak. But before she could say a word, George started to scream. "Yuck! A pigeon just pooped on my head."

Everyone started to laugh, even Katie. In fact, she giggled so hard she couldn't stop. Tears of laughter poured out of her eyes.

George started running around the park, waving his hands wildly. "Get it off! Get it off!" he screamed.

Katie laughed so hard she fell down on the ground. She rolled around on the grass, clutching her side.

"Rosie! Stand up!" Carl shouted. "You're ruining your costume!"

Katie couldn't stop giggling. She tried to stand up, and she tripped over her own feet.

Bam! She fell right into the food table. Her face landed in a lemon meringue pie. Big blobs of yellow and white goo dripped down her cheeks and onto Rosie's costume.

"That's it!" Carl declared. "Wait until the people in California hear about this. You'll never work again, Rosie Moran!"

Chapter 11

That was enough to stop Katie's giggles. She'd ruined Rosie Moran's career!

Katie ran into a nearby trailer and locked the door. Rosie's mother banged on the door. But Katie wouldn't let her in. She didn't want another adult yelling at her.

As she sat alone in Rosie's trailer, Katie understood why Rosie had said she'd needed to take a break and be a normal kid. Acting wasn't all red carpets and famous people. It was memorizing lines, and spending long days on movie sets. There was no time for play-ing—or even laughing.

Just then, Katie felt a cool breeze on the

back of her neck. She looked around. There were no windows in the trailer. And the door was locked tight.

There was only one reason that breeze was blowing.

The magic wind was back!

"Why couldn't you have come ten minutes ago!" Katie shouted angrily.

As if to answer her, the magic wind blew

harder, circling around her like a furious tornado. Katie shut her eyes tight as the wind blew stronger and stronger.

And then, suddenly, it stopped. Slowly, Katie opened her eyes. She wasn't in the trailer anymore. She was back in the park. She looked down. She was wearing her purple jeans again.

"There you are, Katie Kazoo!" George shouted as he, Kevin, Jeremy, and Becky walked toward her.

"Where have you been?" Jeremy asked her. "You missed it."

"Rosie Moran messed up big time!" Kevin laughed. "You should have seen her with that pie in her hair. She looked like she didn't know what had happened."

Katie sighed. Rosie probably had no idea what had happened to her. But Katie did. After all, she was the one who'd really tripped into the food table.

"Serves her right," Becky added.

"Come on, guys, Rosie probably feels awful," Katie argued.

"How do you know?" Becky asked her.

"I know it's not easy being Rosie. I know she works hard. And I know that director is a mean guy," Katie told her.

"How do you know all that?" Jeremy asked.

"Because I . . ." Katie stopped herself. She couldn't tell him how she knew what it was like being Rosie. So instead she said, "I'm sure it wasn't all Rosie's fault."

"That's true," Kevin agreed. "George made her laugh."

"I had pigeon poop in my hair," George insisted.

"It doesn't matter who started it," Jeremy said. "Rosie's career is over."

"Not necessarily . . ." Katie began.

"Uh-oh," Jeremy interrupted. "It sounds like Katie's got another one of her ideas."

Chapter 12

"So tell me again why we want to help Rosie Moran?" Jeremy asked Katie. It was Sunday morning. Rosie was supposed to fly back to California soon. Katie, Jeremy, Suzanne, Becky, Mandy, Miriam, and George were all sitting in the lobby of the Cherrydale Plaza hotel, waiting to catch her before she left.

"Because we were mean to her," Katie said. "We made her feel awful at school."

"But Mrs. Derkman let her dance around the room," George reminded Katie.

"And she acted like Rosie was the only one who could do gymnastics," Becky added.

"So be mad at Mrs. Derkman," Katie said.

"Rosie got me fired from her movie," Suzanne remarked.

Katie shook her head. "No, she didn't. You're the one who did all those goofy things. Rosie didn't even say a word."

Suzanne frowned, but she didn't argue with Katie.

Katie looked at her friends. "So we're all in on the plan?" she asked them.

"Okay, Katie Kazoo, you win," George said.

"Great!" Katie exclaimed. She watched the elevator doors. Finally they opened. Rosie, her mother, and Carl all stepped out at once. Mrs. Moran and Carl both looked angry. Rosie just seemed sad.

"Here goes," Jeremy said. He pulled a pad and pencil from his pocket and raced toward Rosie. "Can I have your autograph?" he asked. "You're my favorite star."

"Jeremy?" Rosie asked.

He nodded. "I can't wait for your next movie."

"You'll be waiting a long time," Carl muttered.

Jeremy took his pad and pencil and ran off. Rosie didn't take two steps before George popped up in front of her.

"Hey, Rosie, remember me?" he asked.

Rosie nodded.

"Do you know when *The Kids Are in Charge* is coming out? I'm thinking of taking some friends to see it for my birthday."

"Well, I don't know if . . ." Rosie began.

"You'll be an old man before I work on that movie again," Carl told George.

"I'm not going to the movie because of you," George said. "As long as Rosie's in it I'll be there."

Carl turned white. His face got all scrunched up. George had really made him mad!

"I'm outta here!" George said as he dashed out of Carl's way.

Rosie, Carl, and Mrs. Moran walked out of the lobby. A big black limo was waiting for them. But before they could get in the car, four girls rushed straight for Rosie.

"Wait, don't go!" Becky cried out. "I never got your autograph."

"Me, neither," Suzanne said. "And I really want it for my scrapbook."

Mandy and Miriam held out their autograph books as well.

Rosie didn't know what to say.

Just then, Katie pushed her way through the crowd of girls. "Boy, you've got so many fans," she told Rosie. "Any movie you make will earn a lot of money."

That got Carl's attention.

"I think it's so brave of you not to want to do *this* movie," Katie said.

Rosie looked at her strangely. "I don't?" she asked.

"Of course you don't," Katie continued. "I mean, it's such a silly script. Isn't that what you told me yesterday?"

Rosie had no idea what Katie was talking about. "I guess," Rosie murmured. "I mean I don't know. I don't really remember a lot about yesterday."

"You don't remember ruining my film?" Carl demanded.

"It's *Rosie's* film," Katie reminded him. "That's why she didn't want to say the stupid words in the script. No kid talks like that."

Carl stared at Rosie. "You don't think the

script is good enough?" he asked.

Rosie gulped. "Well . . . I . . . um . . ."

"Rosie's really smart," Katie interrupted. "You should take her advice and get that script rewritten."

"Hmmm," Carl said. "Let me talk to the studio about this."

As Rosie got into the limo, she looked strangely at Katie. Rosie wasn't quite sure what had just happened. All she knew was that Katie had tried to help her.

That was the kind of thing a real friend would do.

Chapter 13

"Katie, the phone's for you!" Mrs. Carew shouted.

Katie came bounding down the stairs. "Who is it?" she asked her mother.

"Rosie Moran," Mrs. Carew answered. "She's calling from Los Angeles."

Katie was surprised. It had been a month since Rosie had gone back to California. Katie hadn't expected to ever hear from her again.

"Hello," Katie said into the phone.

"Hi, Katie Kazoo!" Rosie answered. "I have great news, and I wanted you to be the first one to know."

"What's up?"

"They're going to rewrite *The Kids Are in Charge*. But it's going to be six months before we can start filming again."

"What are you doing until then?" Katie asked.

"I have to reshoot *The Kids Are in Charge* before I can make another movie. So my mom said I could go to a regular school while we wait!"

"And now you'll have lots of time to make friends," Katie said.

"I hope so," Rosie said. "My mom says from now on I can spend more time with kids my own age. She'll figure out a way for me to work and be more like a regular kid, too."

"That's great!" Katie exclaimed.

"It's all because of you," Rosie admitted. "I'm not sure why you wanted to help me. But I'm glad you did."

Katie didn't know what to say. She couldn't tell Rosie that she'd felt really bad about messing up her career. Rosie would never understand about the magic wind.

"I just wanted to help," she said finally.

The girls talked for a little longer. They exchanged e-mail addresses and promised to write. Katie was very excited. She had a movie star for a pen pal!

As she hung up the phone, Katie felt a cool breeze on the back of her neck. She gulped nervously. Was the magic wind back?

"Katie, please shut the kitchen window," her mother called from the other room. "I think we're going to have a storm."

Katie sighed with relief. It was a regular, everyday wind. She would stay herself . . .

At least for now.

Chapter 14

Tough Tongue Twisters

Actors and actresses learn to speak clearly by saying tongue twisters. Here are some of Rosie Moran's favorites. Can you say each one three times, fast?

Four funny farmers found farming far from fun.

Eight gray geese in a green field grazing.

Six silly sailors set sail on the seven seas.

A glad batch of lads catching crabs.

Six thick thistle sticks.

KATIE KAZOO, SWITCHEROO

For my parents, Gladys and Steve—N.K.

For Julia Andrews—J&W

Text copyright © 2004 by Nancy Krulik. Illustrations copyright © 2004 by John and Wendy. All rights reserved. Published by Grosset & Dunlap, a division of Penguin Young Readers Group, 345 Hudson Street, New York, New York 10014. Printed in the U.S.A.

Library of Congress Cataloging-in-Publication Data

Krulik, Nancy E.
    No messin' with my lesson / by Nancy Krulik ; illustrated by John & Wendy.
        p. cm. — (Katie Kazoo, switcheroo ; 11)
Summary: Katie's teacher, Mrs. Derkman, hopes to win the Teacher of the Year contest, but her chances do not look good when Katie turns into her teacher and cannot keep a class full of out-of-control third-graders in line.
    ISBN 0-448-43357-5 (pbk.)
    [1. School—Fiction. 2. Teachers—Fiction. 3. Contests—Fiction. 4. Magic—Fiction.] I. Title: No messing with my lesson. II. John & Wendy. III. Title.
    PZ7.K9445No 2004
    [Fic]—dc22
                        2003016470
        ISBN 0-448-43357-5   I J

No Messin' with My Lesson

by Nancy Krulik • illustrated by John & Wendy

Grosset & Dunlap

Chapter 1

"Cinderella, dressed in yellow. Went upstairs to kiss a fella. Made a mistake, and kissed a snake. How many doctors did it take? One, two, three . . ."

Katie Carew began to count as she turned her end of the double Dutch jump ropes. Her best friend, Suzanne Lock, was jumping between the ropes. Becky Stern was turning the other end.

Katie's other best friend, Jeremy Fox, was on the soccer field. He was kicking a ball around with Kevin Camilleri and Mandy Banks. George Brennan and Manny Gonzalez were on the swings, laughing at something.

Probably at one of George's jokes.

Everyone was having a great time.

The strange thing was, the only kids on the playground were the kids in class 3A. Everyone else had already gone in to start the school day. But no one had told the kids in Katie's class to stop playing and come inside.

"I wonder where Mrs. Derkman is?" Becky asked.

Usually, their teacher was on the playground before school began. When it was time for classes to start, she would blow her whistle, and the kids would line up to go into the building. But, this morning, Mrs. Derkman was nowhere to be found.

"Do you think we should go inside on our own?" Katie wondered. "School started five minutes ago."

"No way," Suzanne said between jumps. "I'm not going in there until someone tells me I have to."

Just then, Mr. Kane, the school principal, strolled onto the playground. "Class 3A," he called out. "You need to be in school now. Line up."

Katie immediately dropped her end of the double-Dutch ropes, and ran for the door. Suzanne tripped over the fallen ropes. *Plop*. She landed right on her rear end.

"Nice one, Suzanne," George Brennan teased. "How about giving us an instant replay?" He raced past her.

Suzanne glared at George.

As the kids lined up, Jeremy turned to Katie. "Do you think Mrs. Derkman is absent today?" he asked her.

Katie shook her head. "No way. Mrs. Derkman is *never* absent."

"I know," George agreed. "She's *always* at school. She's here when we get here in the morning, and she's here when we leave in the afternoon. I'd swear she lived in the school   if I didn't know she'd moved in next door to you, Katie Kazoo."

The other kids all looked sympathetically at Katie. Imagine having your teacher live right next door. Especially a strict teacher like Mrs. Derkman. Talk about bad luck!

"Maybe she's preparing a surprise for us in the classroom," Miriam Chan suggested.

"Oh, that would be awful," George moaned.

"How do you know?" Miriam asked him. "It could be something great."

"Any surprise Mrs. *Jerk*man could dream up would have to be bad," George told her. George did not like Mrs. Derkman very much.

"You children keep quiet as you walk down the hall," Mr. Kane warned as he led them inside. "The other classes are already busy learning."

$$\times \quad \times \quad \times$$

Sure enough, Mrs. Derkman was there when the kids walked into the room. She was standing in the back of the room, looking through the lens of a video camera. The camera was planted firmly on top of a stand.

"What's that for?" Manny asked Mrs. Derkman.

"I'm going to tape our day," Mrs. Derkman explained.

"Why?" Manny asked.

Mrs. Derkman checked the lens one more time, and then walked to the front of the

room. "After school, I'm going to watch the tapes to see how I teach. That way, I can study what I'm doing right, and what I'm doing wrong. I can come up with ways to be a better teacher."

Katie looked at George. She could tell by the expression on his face that he was practically bursting with ideas for how Mrs. Derkman could be a better teacher. He opened his mouth to say something, but Mrs. Derkman shot him a look. George kept quiet.

"So you're going to watch the tapes the way a coach does after a football game, to see where the team went wrong," Jeremy said.

"Exactly," Mrs. Derkman told him. "You see, I've been entered in the Cherrydale Teacher of the Year Contest. One of the judges is going to come here and watch me teach. I want to make sure that I do my best."

"When is the judge coming?" Kevin asked.

Mrs. Derkman shrugged. "It's a surprise. I don't know when he will come or what he will grade me on."

The kids all stared at their teacher with amazement. Someone was going to give Mrs. Derkman a grade? Now that was a switch!

Mrs. Derkman walked over to the board and picked up a piece of chalk. "Now, just forget about the camera. Pretend it's not there. We have work to do."

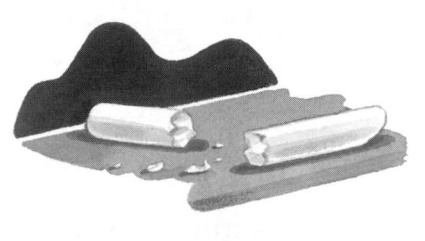

Chapter 2

Mrs. Derkman may not have wanted anyone to think about the camera, but the kids couldn't help it. In fact, it was *all* they could think about.

"Who can tell me one problem the pioneers faced on their trip out west?" Mrs. Derkman asked the class during social studies. Many hands shot up. "Suzanne?" Mrs. Derkman said.

Usually, Suzanne would just give her answer from her seat. But not today. Suzanne stood up. She turned her face to the video camera, reached up, and wiped her forehead. Then she clutched her throat like she was in pain.

"During the summer months, the sun was strong, and sometimes the settlers didn't have enough water to drink," she moaned in a pained voice. "People actually died of thirst." She collapsed on her chair and threw her head back, pretending to faint.

The class began to laugh. A few kids actually applauded. Suzanne stood up and bowed.

"Watch out, Suzanne Superstar is ready for her close-up," Kevin teased.

"Suzanne, sit down," Mrs. Derkman said with a sigh. She looked at the class. "That's true. Both food and water were hard to come by. Now, does anyone else have a thought?"

Katie had some ideas about what problems the pioneers might have had. But she didn't raise her hand. She didn't want to risk giving a wrong answer. If she did, it would be on film forever!

But George wasn't afraid to be on camera. He raised his hand high.

Mrs. Derkman looked around the room to

see if anyone else had a hand up. But George was the only one. "George," Mrs. Derkman said finally.

Like Suzanne, George stood up and turned toward the camera. He held his pencil in his hand, and pretended it was a microphone. "Speaking of westward travel," he said. "Do you know why a drama teacher is like the pony express? Because he's a stage coach!"

A few kids laughed.

"Does anyone know who settled in the west before anyone else?" George continued.

"Who?" Manny asked.

"The sun!" George exclaimed.

The kids all laughed. "Tell another one, George," Kevin shouted.

George grinned. "Why did the criminal carry glue with him when he traveled out west?"

"Why?" Kevin shouted out.

"He wanted to stick up the passengers!"

Everyone laughed . . . everyone but Mrs.

Derkman, that is. "George, this is a classroom, not a comedy club," she scolded.

Mrs. Derkman did not look happy. Her face was all scrunched up, her glasses were halfway down her nose, and she'd squeezed her fist so tight that she'd snapped the chalk in half.

Katie glanced at the video camera in the back of the room. *I wonder how Mrs. Derkman will feel when she sees herself looking like that,* she thought to herself.

Mrs. Derkman didn't turn off her video camera at all during the day. And the more the camera recorded her, the stricter she got. During math time, the kids were all answering multiplication problems in their notebooks. Mrs. Derkman walked around the room, checking their work.

"Mandy, you know that by third grade all of your work has to be written in cursive," Mrs. Derkman scolded her.

Mandy seemed confused. "But this is math," she told her teacher. "There's no such thing as a cursive 7."

Mrs. Derkman continued walking around the room. She stopped in front of the third row. "Class, what is the rule about eating in this room?"

Katie looked around. She didn't see anyone eating anything.

"There is *no* eating in this classroom," Mrs. Derkman said, answering her own question. She strutted over to the window, and stared at

Speedy. "You've been here long enough to know that," she scolded the hamster.

Speedy took one look at Mrs. Derkman's angry face, and leaped away from his food bowl. He ran to hide inside his plastic tube.

The kids stared at their teacher. Worrying about the contest had obviously made her nuts!

"Boy, Mrs. Derkman is in a really bad mood today," Katie whispered to Kevin and Suzanne.

"I'll say," Suzanne agreed. "I think it has to do with that video camera. Some people act strange when there's a camera around."

Katie looked at "Suzanne Superstar" and laughed. "Gee, you think so?"

Chapter 3

Mrs. Derkman finally turned off her camera just before the bell rang. She relaxed right away. So did the kids. "Okay, children," the teacher said, a slight smile returning to her face. "Jeremy is now going to pass out this week's edition of the *Class 3A Times*."

Jeremy stood and proudly began to hand out the newspapers. He really loved being the editor of the class newspaper. "There are lots of great articles this week," he told the other kids. "Like the one about . . ."

"*My* new column is in there," Suzanne interrupted him. "It's called 'Ask Suzanne.' I know everyone is going to love it."

"I can't think of anything I'd want to ask her," Kevin whispered to George.

"I can," George answered. "I want to ask her to go away." Kevin and George laughed.

Suzanne scowled at them. "Shows what you know. I'm going to answer very important questions in my column. This week, I wrote about friendship."

Katie watched as Suzanne argued with

George and Kevin. "Are you sure giving Suzanne her own column was a good idea?" she whispered to Jeremy.

"I needed another article to fill the page," Jeremy admitted.

"But you know Suzanne. This could be trouble," Katie told him.

"It'll be okay," Jeremy answered. "Actually, her advice was pretty good. Read it."

Katie opened the newspaper to page three. Suzanne's column was at the top of the page.

The question was:

Dear Suzanne,

My friend has a pair of pants that she loves to wear. But they are too tight and short on her, and I'm afraid they will split open! I want to tell her, but I don't want her to get mad at me.

Signed,
What Do I Do?

Suzanne had answered:

Dear What Do I Do?:
You should definitely tell your friend that her pants are too small. What if they split in the middle of recess? You will save her from embarrassment. Friends should always be honest with each other. When it comes to friendship, honesty is always the best policy.

"You see," Jeremy said after Katie had read the column. "Suzanne said people should be honest. What trouble could that cause?"

Katie shrugged. "I guess you're right," she agreed.

$$\times \quad \times \quad \times$$

That afternoon, Katie went home and did her homework. Then she went out into her yard to look for her cocker spaniel, Pepper. She found him next door, playing with Mrs. Derkman's dog, Snowball. They were both

sniffing around the tomatoes and cucumbers in Mrs. Derkman's yard.

Katie figured Mrs. Derkman must not be in the yard. Otherwise, she would have shooed the dogs away from her vegetables. Mrs. Derkman loved her garden. She treated her plants like babies. She even sang to them!

Katie was right, Mrs. Derkman wasn't in the garden. But *Mr.* Derkman was. Katie was very surprised. She'd never seen her teacher's husband working in the garden before. He liked to lie in a big hammock under the tree while his wife dug up weeds and planted flowers. But, today, he was the one out there picking fresh cucumbers from the vine.

"Hi, Katie," Mr. Derkman greeted her.

"Hi," Katie replied. "I didn't know you liked to garden."

"I don't," Mr. Derkman admitted. "But my wife is so busy watching her videotapes that she doesn't have time to pick vegetables.

These cucumbers will rot on the vine if I don't bring them in."

"Mrs. Derkman sure is excited about the Teacher of the Year Contest," Katie said.

"I know," Mr. Derkman agreed. "I don't think I've ever seen her this way before. She says if she had only one wish, it would be to win Teacher of the Year."

Katie gulped slightly when Mr. Derkman said that. She knew a lot about wishes. Sometimes, when they came true, they caused a lot of trouble.

Katie learned all about wishes one evening after she'd had a really bad day. She'd lost the football game for her team, ruined her favorite pair of pants, and let out a big burp in front of the whole class. That night, Katie had wished she could be anyone but herself.

There must have been a shooting star overhead when she made that wish, because the very next day, the magic wind came and

turned Katie into Speedy the class hamster! All morning long, she gnawed on chew sticks and ran on a hamster wheel, until she finally turned back into herself!

The magic wind continued to come back again and again. It had already turned Katie into other kids, like Suzanne's baby sister Heather, and her friends Becky Stern and Jeremy Fox. Another time, it turned her into her dog Pepper—and she'd gotten into a huge argument with a particularly nasty squirrel. Once, the wind even turned her into Mr. Kane, the school principal. The whole school was almost destroyed that time!

Katie never knew when the magic wind would come back again. All she knew was that when it did, she was going to wind up getting into some sort of trouble—and so would the person or animal she turned into.

That was why Katie knew it was important to be careful what you wished for!

"Freddy Bear, you have a phone call," Mrs.

Derkman called suddenly from the front door.

Mr. Derkman looked up. "Coming, Snookums," he called back. He turned to Katie. "See you later, kiddo."

Katie sighed as Freddy Bear walked up to the house and went inside with his Snookums. She was *never* going to get used to having Mrs. Derkman as a next-door neighbor.

Chapter 4

"Are you sure it's safe to play in your yard today?" Suzanne asked Katie as they left school with Jeremy and George at the end of the next day. "I don't want to run into Mrs. Derkman."

"Mrs. Derkman's not going to be home yet," Katie assured Suzanne. "And when she does get home, she's not going to bother us. She'll be spending all her time inside watching her videotapes."

"I hope you're right," Jeremy said. "I don't like playing at your house very much now that Mrs. Derkman is your neighbor. I see enough of her at school."

Katie frowned. It made her feel bad that her best friend didn't want to play at her house.

"I was just being honest," Jeremy told her.

The kids began to walk in the direction of Katie's house. A minute later, Becky came up behind them.

Katie jumped. "Becky, you surprised me," Katie exclaimed.

"She didn't surprise *me*," Suzanne said. "She always shows up when Jeremy's around."

Jeremy and Becky both blushed. Then Jeremy looked angry.

"What?" Suzanne asked. "I was just being honest."

Jeremy scowled at Suzanne, but said nothing. What could he say? He was the editor of the class paper. It had been his idea to print Suzanne's advice column in the first place.

"Hi, kids," Mrs. Carew greeted them as they walked up the walkway to Katie's house.

"I hope you're hungry. I've got lots of choco-late chip cookies." She held out a large plate.

Becky grabbed a chocolate chip cookie and took a bite. "This is pretty good, Mrs. Carew," she said. "But my mom makes them much better. Hers are chewier, and they have a lot more chips."

Katie's mom didn't know what to say. The kids all stared at Becky with surprise.

Becky shrugged. "I was just being . . ."

"Honest," George, Jeremy, Suzanne, and Katie finished her sentence for her.

The other kids seemed to like the cookies a lot. They chowed down on them. When they were finished eating, Katie's mom took the empty plate into the house. "Don't stay out here too long," she warned Katie as she went inside. "You have to do your homework."

Katie nodded. "We don't have too much," she assured her mother.

"Does anyone else think Mrs. Derkman is acting especially weird lately?" Suzanne

asked the others once Mrs. Carew was gone and they were alone.

"I'll say," Becky agreed. "Did you hear her yelling at Speedy yesterday?"

"Poor little hamster," Katie agreed.

George stood up. He wrinkled his brow and scrunched up his mouth. He pretended to look through a pair of glasses.

"Speedy, there will be no scratching in this classroom," he said, imitating Mrs. Derkman. "And there will be no running on the hamster wheel. There is no running in the classroom at all. Save that for the playground."

Katie giggled.

"No laughing, Katie," George said in a stern voice. "School is not supposed to be fun."

"It sure wasn't fun today," Jeremy said. "I was afraid to breathe."

"That's the new rule," George said. "From now on, students are only allowed to breathe during lunch."

The kids all laughed. George was imitating their teacher perfectly.

"That's pretty good, George," Jeremy giggled.

"Yeah, you sound just like Mrs. *Jerk*man," Suzanne agreed.

Suddenly, the kids heard footsteps on the sidewalk. They stopped laughing and turned around.

"Uh-oh," Becky murmured.

Mrs. Derkman was standing in her driveway. She had just arrived home from school. Katie was sure her teacher had heard them talking about her.

"We're in trouble now," George whispered.

But Mrs. Derkman didn't say a word. She just turned, and sadly went into her house.

Chapter 5

When Katie arrived at school the next morning, everyone was upset. And not because of how strict Mrs. Derkman had become. The kids were fighting with one another—and it was all because of Suzanne's advice column.

"I don't know what your problem is," Katie heard Jeremy say to Manny. "All I said was that you don't run fast enough to be on our team in the relay race."

"That's really mean," Manny replied.

"I'm just being honest," Jeremy told him. "You're not a fast runner. As your friend, I owe it to you to tell you the truth."

Jeremy and Manny weren't the only ones having an argument. George and Kevin weren't getting along too well, either.

"Here's my new joke," George said. "What do you call a jogging almond?"

"What?" Kevin asked.

"A health nut!" George laughed, but Kevin didn't.

George looked at him strangely. "Don't you get it?"

Kevin nodded. "I get it. I just don't think it's funny."

George's eyes opened wide. "What do you mean it's not funny?" he demanded.

"Hey, don't get mad at me," Kevin insisted. "I'm just being honest."

George stormed away.

It wasn't only the boys who were having trouble with the truth. As she turned away from George, Katie spotted Zoe Canter sitting under a tree. She was crying. Katie walked over to see what was wrong.

"What's up, Zoe?" she asked.

"Miriam and Mandy just told me not to meet them at the mall on Saturday," Zoe told Katie between sobs.

"Why would they do that?"

Zoe shrugged. "They said they *honestly* wanted some time alone. Now *I* have nothing to do. I can't believe they're leaving me out like this."

Katie sighed. The kids were taking Suzanne's advice too seriously. Sometimes, the truth hurt. Katie decided to talk to Suzanne about it. Maybe her friend could write a new article for next week's paper— one that was about not hurting other people's feelings.

But, before Katie could speak to Suzanne, Mrs. Derkman blew her whistle three times. It was time to go inside.

The kids were still arguing as they walked into the classroom, put their homework in the

bin, and hung up their jackets. As soon as everyone was in their seats, Mrs. Derkman called for quiet.

"You have to be especially well-behaved now," Mrs. Derkman reminded the class. "The judges for the Teacher of the Year Contest will be here any day now. It could be today, tomorrow, or the next day."

"You mean we have to be good for three whole days?" George asked. "I don't know if I can do that."

Mrs. Derkman didn't say anything. She didn't have to. The look on her face was enough to make George be quiet.

"She's in a bad mood again!" Suzanne mumbled under her breath.

Unfortunately, she wasn't so quiet that Mrs. Derkman couldn't hear her. The teacher's face got even more angry. She stared at the second row. "Did you say something . . . Katie?" she asked.

"No," Katie assured her honestly.

"Yes, you did," Mrs. Derkman said. "I heard you."

"It wasn't me," Katie insisted. "It was . . ." Katie stopped herself. She didn't want to squeal on Suzanne.

"There is no rudeness allowed in this class. Go down and sit in Mr. Kane's office," Mrs. Derkman told her. "You need to spend some time thinking about how your words affect others."

"But I . . ."

"No buts, Katie. I said go to Mr. Kane's office."

Katie could feel tears welling up in her eyes. She was being punished, and she hadn't done anything wrong. That was the worst feeling in the world.

The hallway was empty as Katie made her way toward the principal's office. Suddenly, she felt a cool, gentle breeze blowing on the back of her neck. She looked up to see if a window was open. But all the windows in the

hallway were shut tight. So were the doors. The breeze wasn't coming from outside.

Oh, no! The magic wind was back!

Within seconds, the wind began to swirl around Katie like a wild tornado, blowing her hair all around her face. Katie shut her eyes tight. The wind grew stronger—so strong that Katie thought it would blow her away!

And then it stopped. Just like that. The magic wind was gone.

Which could only mean one thing. Katie had turned into someone else. The question was, who?

Chapter 6

"What page should we turn to, Mrs. Derkman?" Katie heard someone ask.

Slowly, she opened her eyes. She looked around. The room was very familiar. There was a hamster by the window, rows of desks, and a bulletin board that said "Math Rules!" on the back wall.

Katie knew this classroom very well. This was her classroom. Class 3A.

Okay, so now she knew where she was. But she didn't know *who* she was.

"Mrs. Derkman," Mandy said again. "You didn't tell us what page to turn to."

All eyes seemed to be on Katie. Katie looked down at the floor. There were sensible

leather shoes on her feet. She was wearing a black skirt that just covered her knees, and a long-sleeved white blouse. Katie would never wear boring clothes like that.

But Mrs. Derkman would!

Oh, no! Katie had turned into her teacher!

Katie gulped. She didn't know anything about being a teacher. She didn't even know what book the kids had on their desks. She'd been in the hall when Mrs. Derkman had started the lesson.

But there was one person who knew how to be Mrs. Derkman. And he did it perfectly. Katie thought back to yesterday, when George had imitated Mrs. Derkman. She tried to do what he had done. She wrinkled her brow, and scrunched up her mouth. She looked down through Mrs. Derkman's half-glasses.

"Mrs. Derkman, do you have a toothache?" Miriam Chan asked her.

Katie sighed. Obviously, she didn't look as much like Mrs. Derkman as she'd thought. She was never going to be able to teach her friends anything.

But she had to do *something* with the class. Otherwise, they were sure to figure out that

she wasn't really their teacher. Katie thought for a moment. Then she came up with a plan.

"Class, I've changed my mind," Katie said finally. "We're going to start the day with free reading. Everyone, take out your books."

The kids all looked at one another. They never started the day with free reading.

"What are you waiting for?" Katie scolded them, trying to sound like Mrs. Derkman. "Take out your books."

The kids did as they were told. As they began to read, Katie sat down at Mrs. Derkman's desk. The blue notebook Mrs. Derkman always carried was sitting right there. Maybe there was some clue in there about what Mrs. Derkman had wanted to teach today.

Katie opened the notebook. On the first page was a list of the kids in class 3A. Next to each of the names was a row of letters. She looked at the first one.

Kevin Camilleri: B, B+, A, C

Katie slammed the book shut. The blue book was Mrs. Derkman's grade book. Katie didn't want to look at her friends' test grades. Well, maybe she *wanted* to, but she knew she shouldn't. Grades were private.

Katie sat back in Mrs. Derkman's big, wooden chair and sighed. Her only hope was that the magic wind would blow again and turn her back into herself before she actually had to teach anything.

The trouble with that plan was that the magic wind only came when Katie was alone. Teachers were never alone in school. There were always kids around them. Teachers never even got to go to the bathroom. At least, Katie had never seen one get up to go.

As Katie thought about her big problem, she heard whispering. She looked out at her friends. Becky was whispering something to Jeremy.

"Becky!" Katie scolded her, trying to sound like their teacher. "We are reading now."

Becky looked back down at her book.

One minute later, Katie watched as a note flew across the room and landed on Zoe's desk. Katie knew that Mrs. Derkman would take the note and read it out loud. But Katie couldn't be that mean.

"Zoe, throw that in the garbage right now," she said instead.

Zoe stood up and did as she was told.

After that, everyone was quiet. At least for a few minutes. Then Kevin started drumming his fingers on his desk. *Tap tap tap. Tap tap tap.*

George began humming as he read. *Hmmm. Hmmm. Hmmm.*

The sound was driving Katie crazy. "Kevin! George!" she shouted, her voice suddenly sounding shrill and sharp. "This isn't music class. There's no singing or drumming here. You need to be quiet."

"Boy, Mrs. *Jerk*man is really mean today," Mandy whispered to Suzanne.

Katie frowned. She hadn't been trying to be mean. She'd just been trying to make sure everyone could read. Obviously, free reading time wasn't working. Katie was going to have to teach a lesson whether she liked it or not.

She wrote a division problem on the board.

$$3\overline{)15}$$

"Okay, class, put away your books," Katie said. "We're going to have a math lesson. Today, we will review division."

It was better to review something than to teach something new. After all, Katie didn't know anything new.

"Fifteen divided by three is five," Jeremy said.

"Very good," Katie agreed.

"That's not good," Suzanne interrupted.

"It's not?" Katie asked her.

"No. He called out. We're not allowed to call out," Suzanne explained.

Oops. Suzanne was right. Mrs. Derkman did not allow anyone to answer a question without raising his or her hand.

"So what?" Becky butted in. "He was right, wasn't he?"

"But he didn't follow the rules," Suzanne said.

"Well, neither did you," Jeremy told her. "You just called out, too."

Before Katie could say anything, Mr. Kane entered the room. He was followed by a stranger in a blue suit. The stranger was carrying a notebook. The two men walked quietly to the back of the room. Mr. Kane smiled and whispered something to the visitor.

Suddenly, Katie had a horrible thought. The stranger must be the judge for the Teacher of the Year Contest. He was going to judge Mrs. Derkman right now. And Mrs. Derkman wasn't even there!

This was *so* not good.

Chapter 7

There was nothing Katie could do but keep on teaching. Quickly, she scribbled another division problem on the board.

"Who can answer this question?" Katie asked the class. "What is twenty-seven divided by nine?" Lots of kids raised their hands. "Kevin?" Katie said.

"Four," Kevin said confidently.

Katie nodded and turned to the blackboard. She began to write another problem on the board.

But, before she could, Mandy raised her hand. "Mrs. Derkman?"

"Yes, Mandy?" Katie asked.

"Kevin's not right," Mandy told her. "Twenty-seven divided by nine equals three."

"It does not," Kevin argued.

"Sure it does," Mandy told him. "Because nine times three equals twenty-seven."

"Uh, very good, Mandy. I must have heard Kevin incorrectly," muttered Katie.

Mandy smiled at Katie. "I know all my times tables perfectly, Mrs. Derkman."

"You're stuck-up," Kevin said.

"That's not nice," Miriam chimed in.

"I'm just being honest, like Suzanne said we should be," Kevin told her.

"You're jealous because I'm better in math and sports than you are," Mandy told him.

"You're not so great, Mandy," Becky butted in. "You're not the best soccer player in the class. Jeremy is. And that's the honest truth!"

Katie knew she had to calm the kids down. But how? "You guys, come on," she said help-lessly.

No one listened to her. Instead, the

arguing got worse. "Becky, you always say things like that," Suzanne said. "Everyone knows you have a big, fat crush on Jeremy."

Jeremy blushed. He turned to Suzanne. "Well, as long as we're being honest," he said, "you look like a banana in that yellow dress!"

Suzanne gulped. No one had ever said anything bad about her clothes before. "I do not!" she shouted. "This is a very cool outfit. Everybody thinks so."

"I don't," Becky said. "I think Jeremy is right. You *do* look like a banana."

"You don't know anything about style," Suzanne shouted back.

"You think you're the best at everything," Becky said to Suzanne.

"I do not!" Suzanne shouted back.

"I'm just telling the truth," Becky said. "But you're not the best. Can you do this?" Becky leaped out of her seat and did a back flip. She landed on the floor in a split.

Katie looked helplessly at the class. She

gulped. Mr. Kane was still standing there in the back of the room. But he didn't look happy anymore. His face was beet red, and his eyes were bulging. A vein was throbbing at the top of his bald head.

The principal couldn't take the arguing anymore. He took a step toward the front of the room and opened his mouth to speak.

But, before Mr. Kane could say a word, the judge tapped him on the shoulder. He whispered something in the principal's ear. Mr. Kane whispered something back. The judge shook his head.

Mr. Kane threw his hands up in the air. "This is a disaster!" he said. Then he stormed out of the room. The door slammed shut behind him.

The judge did not leave the room. He stayed to watch what would happen next. From the look on his face, Katie could tell he was very disappointed at the way things were going. So, Katie did a very un-Derkman thing.

She leaped up on a desk and whistled—loud.

The kids stopped talking and stared at their teacher. Mrs. Derkman had never done anything like that before.

"Okay, everyone sit down," Katie said. "This is not a nice way to act."

"But we're just being honest," Suzanne said. "Friends have to be honest with each other."

Katie nodded. "There's a difference between being honest, and being mean," she said. "I think maybe you were using Suzanne's advice column as an excuse to be mean. And that is totally not okay."

Totally not okay? The kids all stared at one another. Mrs. Derkman never spoke like that.

"I think it's okay to be honest if you're trying to help someone. But you should do that in private. And sometimes it's better to keep quiet than to say something that'll hurt your friend's feelings. You guys didn't care whose feelings you hurt."

The class stared at her. Mrs. Derkman never called her class *you guys*. She always called them children or students. Mrs. Derkman sure was acting strange.

But she was right. And the kids knew it.

At first, no one said anything. Then, Mandy turned to Kevin. "I guess it wasn't nice to say you weren't good in math or sports. You're really good at basketball."

Kevin nodded. "Thanks. And you're amazing in math. I guess I was just mad that I got the problem wrong."

Katie smiled at the class. "I think we should put our math books away. I have a better lesson." She began to hand out pieces of paper. "I want each of you to make a list of everyone in this class. Then I want you to write one nice thing about each of your class-mates."

"I'll start with George. He's really funny," Jeremy said as he began his list.

"Suzanne has great style," Becky said, writing on her paper. "And Jeremy is an awesome soccer player."

"Zoe is a terrific artist," Miriam added as she wrote.

"Manny has good handwriting," Suzanne murmured as she began to make up her list.

Before long, the kids were all busy writing. Katie looked back at the contest judge. He seemed really happy to see the students interested in their work!

But would that be enough for Mrs. Derkman to win the contest?

Chapter 8

Somehow, Katie managed to get through the rest of the day as Mrs. Derkman. When school ended, she was really tired. Keeping a whole class of third-graders busy and out of trouble wasn't easy. Katie just wanted to go home and relax.

But which home should she go to? She couldn't go to her house. Not as long as she looked like Mrs. Derkman. As she walked home, Katie began to worry. This was the longest she'd ever spent as someone else.

Katie hoped the magic wind would come back soon. If it didn't, Katie might wind up eating dinner with Freddy Bear Derkman!

Just then, the door to Mrs. Derkman's house swung open. But it wasn't the magic wind that did it. It was Mr. Derkman.

"Surprise, Snookums," he called out as he walked toward Katie. "I got out of work early."

"Oh, hello, Mr. Derk . . ." Katie began. "I mean, Freddy Bear."

Mr. Derkman reached out his arms. "How about a kissy-poo, Snookums?" he asked. He puckered up his lips for a big smooch.

Yuck! Katie certainly didn't want to give Freddy Bear a kissy-poo! But how could she avoid it?

"Ruff! Ruff!" Just then, Pepper came running over to Katie. He rubbed his back up against her knees and barked happily. Katie bent down and scratched him gratefully behind the ears.

Pepper licked Katie on the nose. He knew she wasn't *really* Mrs. Derkman. Pepper would know his Katie anywhere.

But Snowball didn't know who Katie was. She ran up and sniffed at Katie. Then she looked up, confused. This person looked like her human mommy, she smelled like her human mommy, but somehow Snowball knew that she wasn't Mrs. Derkman. Snowball began to bark wildly.

"I guess she's hungry," Mr. Derkman said. "I'll take her inside and give her some food."

As Mr. Derkman went back into the house, Katie breathed a sigh of relief. Thank

goodness for dogs. But Katie knew she couldn't avoid kissing Mr. Derkman forever—at least not as long as she was *Mrs*. Derkman.

Just then, Katie felt a cool breeze blowing on the back of her neck. Katie looked up at the trees. The leaves were still. She looked down at the grass. Not a blade was moving.

The magic wind was back.

Within seconds, the wind was swirling around her like a giant tornado. Katie felt like she could be blown away at any minute. Quickly, she grabbed onto a tree and shut her eyes, tight.

And then it stopped. Just like that.

Slowly, Katie opened her eyes. She looked down at her feet. The sensible leather shoes were gone, and there were platform sneakers in their place. Instead of a skirt, Katie was wearing jeans, with laces down the sides. She put her hands to her face. She wasn't wearing glasses anymore.

Just then, Katie's mother came outside.

"There you are, Katie," her mother said. "How was school?"

Katie smiled brightly. She was back! "School was okay," she said.

"Anything exciting happen?"

Katie knew she couldn't tell her mother what had happened today. Her mother wouldn't believe her. Katie wouldn't have believed it either, if it hadn't happened to her.

"Nah," Katie said finally. "It was just a regular day."

Chapter 9

Most of the kids in class 3A were already on the playground by the time Katie arrived at school the next day. But they weren't playing or running around. They were busy watching as Mr. Kane spoke to Mrs. Derkman. The principal did not look happy.

"Your class was out of control yesterday," he told Mrs. Derkman.

"I know," Mrs. Derkman admitted sadly. "I'm not sure how that happened."

"What do you mean?" Mr. Kane asked.

"Well, I mean, I know what happened. But it's almost like that wasn't me up there in the front of the room." Mrs. Derkman sounded very confused.

"It certainly looked like you," Mr. Kane told her.

"It was me," Mrs. Derkman said. "I mean, at least I think it was. But I didn't feel like me. Oh, I don't know what to think."

Mr. Kane shook his head. "Well, it doesn't matter now. It doesn't seem as though you'll be winning the Teacher of the Year Award this time around."

Mrs. Derkman looked like she was about to cry.

$$\times \quad \times \quad \times$$

"Boy, Mrs. Jerkman looks unhappy. Mr. Kane must be really mad at her," George told the other kids.

"That's not nice, George," Katie said.

"What?" George asked her.

"Calling her Mrs. Jerkman," Katie told him.

"We always call her that," Kevin said.

"It's still not nice."

The other kids stared at Katie. *Was she*

really standing up for their teacher?

"Mrs. Derkman isn't nice to us, either," Suzanne reminded Katie. "She's very strict. And she gets mad a lot."

"That's because we're not always very good in class," Katie reminded her. "We pass notes and whisper."

"Yeah, well, Mrs. Derkman writes notes, too," George argued. "She sent one to my mother last week. And it wasn't a nice note, either!"

Katie rolled her eyes. "What about yesterday?" she asked the kids. "Everybody was yelling at each other during math. The judge from that contest saw the whole fight."

"How do you know what happened?" George asked Katie. "You were in Mr. Kane's office all day."

Of course, Katie *had* been in the classroom. But she couldn't tell the other kids that. So, instead, she said, "I heard about it. It sounds like everyone was mad at each other."

"But we made up," Mandy told Katie. "And we wrote nice things about each other. The judge from the contest saw us doing that, too."

"Yeah, he seemed happy about that," Miriam added. "He was really smiling when he left."

Katie shrugged. "But he wasn't happy enough to make Mrs. Derkman the Teacher of the Year. She really wanted that award. We blew it for her."

"She blew it for herself," George said. "She jumped up on a desk and whistled. If I did that, she'd send me to the principal's office."

"Yeah," Kevin agreed.

Katie gulped. George was right. Maybe if she hadn't jumped up on that desk, Mrs. Derkman would have had a chance. Now Katie felt worse than ever. "Mrs. Derkman deserves that award. She works really hard. Her feet hurt at the end of the day," Katie insisted.

Jeremy looked at her strangely. "How do you know?" he asked.

"I . . . er . . . well, she stands up at the board so much, I just figure they would hurt," Katie said quickly. "Besides, Mrs. Derkman might not be the nicest teacher in the school, but we learn a lot with her. We're the only class who studied geography this year. And we're the only ones who got to do research projects on things that interested us."

The kids couldn't argue with that. They *had* learned a lot in third grade. For a minute, everyone was quiet.

"We should make it up to her," Mandy said finally.

"I'm going to try to be extra good today," Miriam vowed.

"Me, too," Zoe agreed.

"I guess I will, too," Kevin said. He turned to Suzanne. "That means you can't ask me to pass any notes to Katie."

"I won't," Suzanne agreed. "I'm not going to write any notes today."

It sounded like everyone was going to try to make Mrs. Derkman happy today. Everyone except George, that is. He hadn't said anything about being good in class. All the kids turned to look at him.

"Why are you all staring at me?" George asked.

"Because we want you to be nice to Mrs. Derkman today," said Miriam.

"Yeah," agreed Zoe.

"That means no jokes, George," Kevin said, laughing.

"Oh, boy," replied George.

"George, please be nice to Mrs. Derkman today," Katie pleaded.

George sighed. "Do I have to?"

"Come on, George," Kevin said. "If I have to be good, so do you. Besides, it will really freak her out if *you're* good."

George smiled brightly. He liked that idea.

"Okay," he agreed. "But just for today."

Katie looked at her friends and grinned. Mrs. Derkman wasn't going to get a big trophy. But she was going to have an easy day teaching class 3A. Surely that would make her happy.

Chapter 10

The kids were all true to their word. No one spoke without raising their hand. No one passed any notes in class. No one chewed gum, or stared at the clock, or doodled in their notebook.

But Mrs. Derkman didn't seem to notice how well her students were behaving. She just frowned and sighed a lot.

At the end of the day, Mrs. Derkman told the kids to open their free reading books. Usually, Mrs. Derkman watched the kids as they read to make sure no one misbehaved. But today, Mrs. Derkman stared out the window. She didn't seem to notice the class at all.

Suddenly, there was a knock at the door. Mr. Kane walked into the classroom. He was carrying a gold trophy.

Mrs. Derkman turned and looked at him in confusion. "What is this for?" she asked. "I don't understand."

"This is for you," Mr. Kane said. "It's from the Cherrydale Teacher of the Year Award Committee."

"But you said I didn't win," Mrs. Derkman reminded him.

"You didn't win Teacher of the Year. That went to a teacher at the middle school."

"Then what is that trophy for?" Mrs. Derkman asked him.

"It's a special award," Mr. Kane said. "It's the first time they've ever given it."

"What's it for?" Katie asked excitedly, forgetting that she wasn't supposed to call out in class.

Mrs. Derkman must have forgotten that rule, too. She didn't yell at Katie. Instead she

asked, "Yes, what is it for?"

Mr. Kane looked at the plaque on the base of the trophy. *"This award is presented to Mrs. Barbara Derkman for her creative lesson on consideration and caring for one another's feelings,"* he read.

Katie smiled. She *knew* the judge had liked that part of the class.

Mr. Kane gave Mrs. Derkman her trophy. "The contest judge called to tell me he liked the way you were able to get your students to apologize and see the good in one another," he said. Then he added, "Asking the students to write nice things about each of their class-mates was a great idea."

"Oh," Mrs. Derkman said. "I guess you're talking about that pile of papers on my desk."

"You sound like you don't know where those papers came from," Mr. Kane laughed.

Mrs. Derkman didn't say anything. The truth was, she *wasn't* completely sure about anything that had happened yesterday.

"Anyway, he was really impressed with the way you were able to talk to your students on their own level. He said you almost sounded like a third-grader yourself."

Katie choked back a laugh. Mrs. Derkman had sounded like a third-grader yesterday because she *was* a third-grader. But, of course, Katie was the only one who knew that. And she wasn't going to tell anyone.

"I'm sure your class is very proud of you,"

Mr. Kane told Mrs. Derkman. He started to clap for her. The kids clapped, too.

"I'm proud of them," Mrs. Derkman told Mr. Kane. "I may not be the teacher of the year, but 3A is definitely Cherrydale's Class of the Year. To celebrate, I'm not giving any homework today. I want you all to go home and play!"

The class cheered even louder.

"Does this mean we can stop being good now?" George whispered to Katie as the class cheered for their teacher.

Before Katie could answer him, she felt a cool breeze on the back of her neck. *Oh, no! Was the magic wind back again? Was it going to change her into someone else right here in front of all her friends?* The magic wind had never come when other people were around before. But there was a first time for everything.

"Katie, you'd better close that window," Mrs. Derkman said. "That wind isn't good for

Speedy. He might catch a cold."

Katie breathed a sigh of relief. If Mrs. Derkman felt the breeze, then the magic wind hadn't come back. At least not right now. But it could come back anytime, and turn Katie into anyone.

She hurried to close the window. She never knew who the wind might turn her into next. It could turn her into Speedy again! And the last thing Katie would want to be turned into was a hamster with a cold.

For now, though, Katie was herself. And that made her very happy. After all, of all the people the magic wind had turned her into so far, Katie Carew was the one she liked best.

An Apple for the Teacher

This apple graham cracker snacker is a snack even Mrs. Derkman can't resist.

You will need:
2 red delicious apples
1 cup lemon juice
$1/2$ cup chunky peanut butter
2 tablespoons honey
$1/2$ tsp. cinnamon
6 whole graham crackers
A helpful adult

Here's what you do: Ask an adult to core the apples and cut each one in half. Then cut

each half into three wedges (so you have 12 apple wedges). Dip the wedges in lemon juice to keep them from browning. Place the wedges in a single layer on a microwavable plate or baking dish. Cover the wedges loosely with waxed paper. Ask an adult to microwave the wedges on high for 3 $\frac{1}{2}$–4 minutes (until apples are tender). Drain the apples on a paper towel.

In a small bowl, combine the peanut butter, honey, and cinnamon. Snap the graham crackers in half to make 12 squares. Spread a layer of the peanut butter mixture on each of the six graham cracker squares. Top each square with the remaining graham cracker squares to make sandwiches.

Makes six snacks.